a boy and his bunny

a boy and

his bunny

by sean bryan

illustrations by tom murphy

ARCADE PUBLISHING / NEW YORK

One day
a boy woke up
with a bunny
on his head.

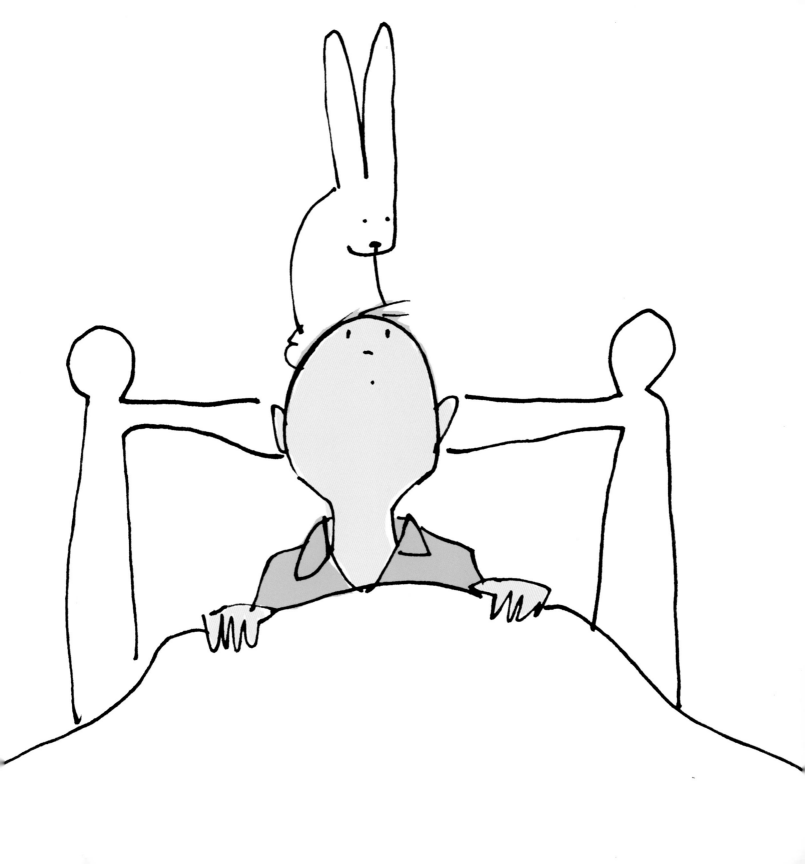

He named him Fred,
this bunny on his head.

"Good morning," said Fred, the bunny on his head.

And the boy

got out of

bed with

you-know-who

on his head.

His mother
cooked
breakfast,
made sure
he was fed.

The boy
ate quite a bit...

...but he saved
some for Fred.

Mother looked puzzled as she brought him his bread.

"You know, I hate to tell you, but it's got to be said…"

"You have

a great

big

bunny

on your

head!"

"And what's wrong with that?" asked the big bunny Fred. "You can do anything with a bunny on your head."

Books
can be read
with a bunny
on your head.

Peanut butter
can be spread
with a bunny
on your head.

Oui, oui, French can be said with a bunny on your head.

Even armies can be led with
a bunny on your head.

"And not only that,"
the boy said to Fred,

"you could
ride a bobsled
with a bunny
on your head."

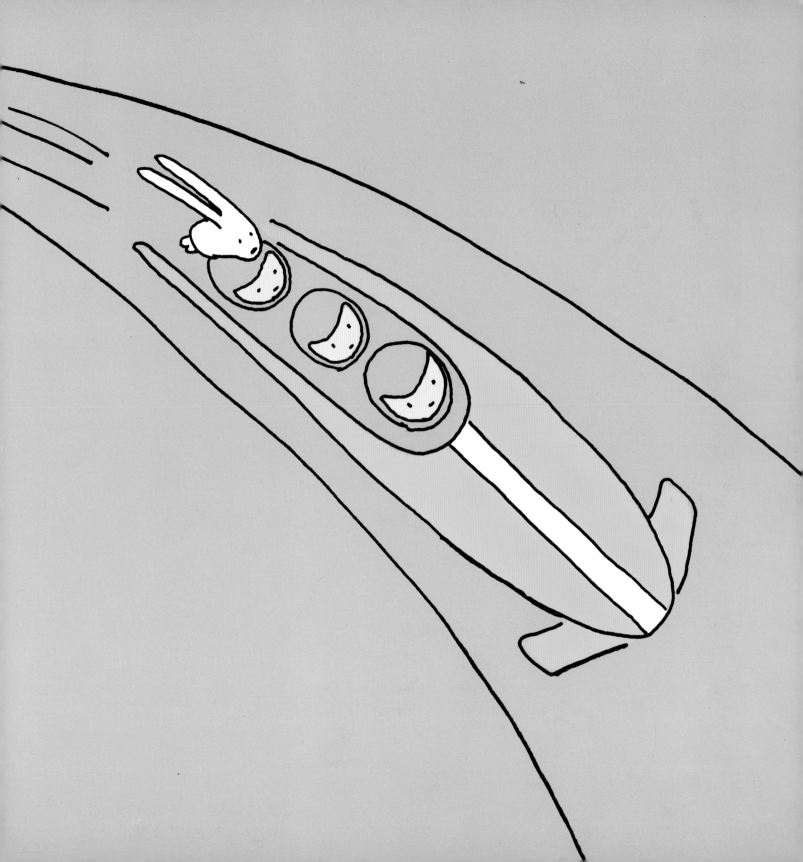

You could build a tool shed
with a bunny on your head.

You could drive a moped with a bunny on your head.

Or explore the seabed

with a bunny on your head.

"Wow,"
said the boy's mother,
"I take back what I said."

"You look pretty cool
with that bunny on your head."

But what would she think
a few minutes later,

when his sister walked in
with a small alligator?

For Henry Hobbs, a very imaginative boy — SB

For my little one — TM

Text copyright © 2005 by Sean Bryan
Illustrations copyright © 2005 by Tom Murphy

FIRST EDITION

Library of Congress Cataloging-in-Publication Data

Bryan, Sean
   A boy and his bunny / by Sean Bryan ; illustrated by Tom Murphy. — 1st ed.
      p. cm.
   Summary: One morning, a boy wakes up with a rabbit on his head and,
although his mother is skeptical, he soon discovers that he can be fed,
ride a bobsled, and even look cool with a rabbit on his head.
   ISBN 1-55970-725-9
   [1. Rabbits — Fiction. 2. Humorous stories. 3. Stories in rhyme.] I. Murphy, Tom 1972– ill. II. Title.

PZ8.3.B829Bo 2005
[E] — dc22   2003027334

Published in the United States by Arcade Publishing, Inc., New York
Distributed by Time Warner Book Group

Visit our Web site at www.arcadepub.com

10 9 8 7 6 5 4 3 2 1

Designed by Tom Murphy

Imago / PRINTED IN CHINA